C29 0000 0857 198

D1581045

Look Up at the Stars

For Florence and Bump
— K.C.

For Maura
— M.A.L.

Brimming with creative inspiration, how-to projects, and useful information to enrich your everyday life, Quarto Knows is a favourite destination for those pursuing their interests and passions. Visit our site and dig deeper with our books into your area of interest: Quarto Creates, Quarto Cooks, Quarto Homes, Quarto Lives, Quarto Drives, Quarto Explores, Quarto Gifts, or Quarto Kids.

Text © 2019 Katie Cotton. Illustrations © 2019 Miren Asiain Lora.
First published in 2019 by Frances Lincoln Children's Books.
First published in paperback in 2021 by Frances Lincoln Children's Books, an imprint of The Quarto Group.
The Old Brewery, 6 Blundell Street, London N7 9BH.
T (0)20 7700 6700 F (0)20 7700 8066 www.QuartoKnows.com

The right of Katie Cotton to be identified as the author and Miren Asiain Lora to be identified
as the illustrator of this work has been asserted by them in accordance with the
Copyright, Designs and Patents Act, 1988 (United Kingdom).
All rights reserved.
No part of this publication may be reproduced, stored in a retrieval system, or transmitted, in any form,
or by any means, electrical, mechanical, photocopying, recording or otherwise without the prior
written permission of the publisher or a licence permitting restricted copying.

A catalogue record for this book is available
from the British Library.
ISBN 978-1-78603-773-2
The illustrations were created using watercolour
Set in Print Clearly
Designed by Zoë Tucker
Production by Dawn Cameron

Manufactured in Guangdong, China CC072021
1 3 5 7 9 8 6 4 2

Frances Lincoln
First Editions

Katie Cotton & Miren Asiain Lora

Look Up at the Stars

Come close, my sweet child,
let's hug really tight.
Look up at the stars
that sparkle, so bright.

Mum, look at the stars
that shine above me.
If I could hold one
how happy I'd be!

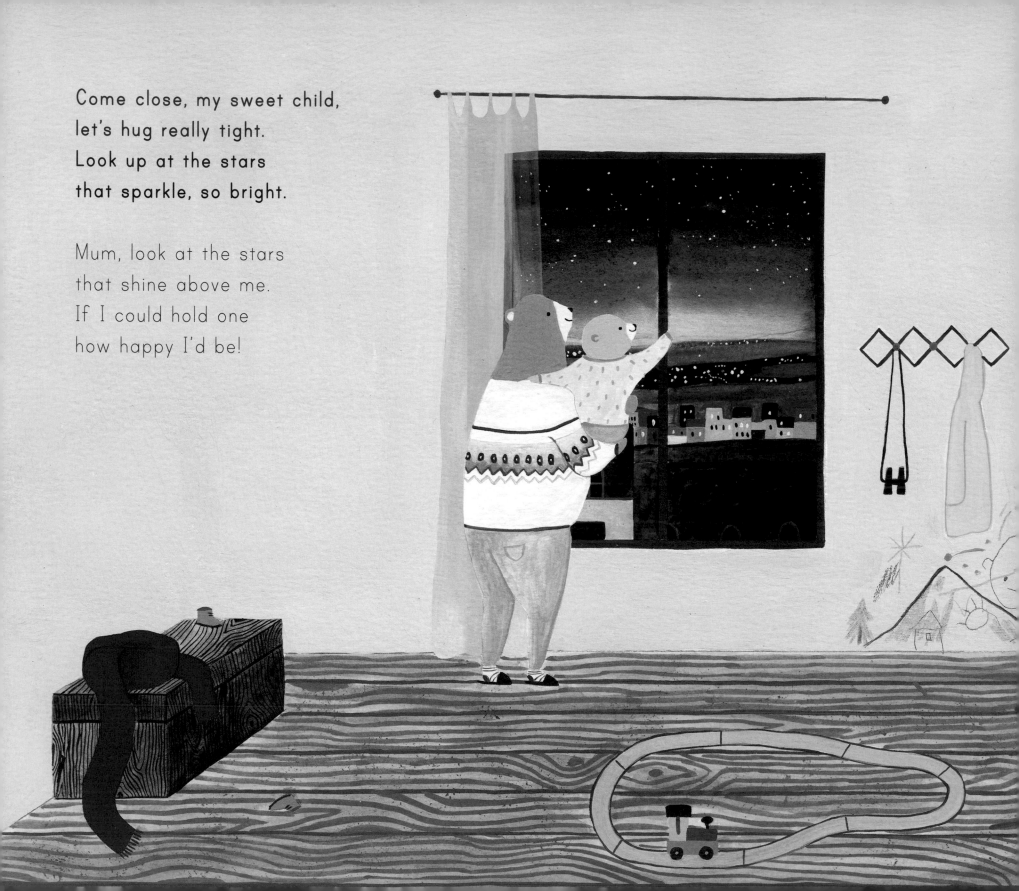

I'll catch you a star,
my darling, my love.
I'll catch you a star
from the sky up above.

Let's go to the top
of Mount Digger-Doo.
That's where I'll catch
a star just for you.

We'll go through the woods
as night ends the day.
Through hallways of trees
we'll keep on our way.

While shadows and rustles
might give us a fright,
and roots make us stumble,

the stars give us light.

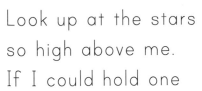

Look up at the stars
so high above me.
If I could hold one
how happy I'd be!

I'll catch you a star,
my darling, my dear.
I'll catch you a star
so you'll never feel fear.

We'll sail across seas
where waves crash and roar.
At times it may seem
we'll never reach shore.
But when our sailboat
is thrown to great heights,
we'll never give up:

the stars give us light.

Look up at the stars
so high above me.
If I could hold one
how happy I'd be!

I'll catch you a star,
my darling, my child.
I'll catch you a star
so you'll always smile.

We'll trample through snow
that's icy and sweet
and try to ignore
the cold in our feet.

And though we are tired
and we want to stop,
we won't 'till the sign...

says we're at the top.

Look up at the stars
so high above me.
If I could hold one
how happy I'd be!

I'll catch you a star,

my darling, my love.

I'll catch you a star
from the sky up...

I'm sorry, my love.
I can't catch a star.
The sky is too high,
I can't reach that far.
So now let's go home.
It's dark and it's late.

Don't leave just yet, Mum.
I see something... wait!

Look down at the stars,
the lights in the night.
They chase away dark
and sparkle so bright.

Look down at the stars,
so low below me.
Look down at our lane
and see what I see.

Yes, there in our house
a light softly gleams.

It takes away fear
and it brightens our dreams.

We have our own star
and it's waiting below.
It's shining so strongly,

we just didn't know.

Katie Cotton studied English at Oxford University before becoming an editor and critically acclaimed author of children's books. She lives and works in London. Her previous titles include *Dear Bunny*, illustrated by Blanca Gomez, *Counting Lions*, illustrated by Stephen Walton, and *The Road Home*, illustrated by Sarah Jacoby.

Miren Asiain Lora was born in Pamplona, Spain and now lives in Buenos Aires, Argentina. Her artwork has been shown in several exhibitions in Spain, Argentina and Mexico. Her works convey the magic of everyday life, the charm of little moments that hold a secret to be deciphered. She illustrated *Look Up at the Stars* as a gift for her first daughter.